CLICK, CLACK, Splish, Splash

A Counting Adventure

by doreen cronin
and
betsy lewin

SCHOLASTIC INC.

New York Toronto London Auckland Sydney
Mexico City New Delhi Hong Kong Buenos Aires

1 farmer sleeping.

2 feet creeping.

3 buckets piled high.

4
chickens
standing
by.

5 cows type a note.

6 goats load the boat.

7 pigs lead the way.

8 sheep decide to stay.

9

mice
leave
a
note
on
the
door.

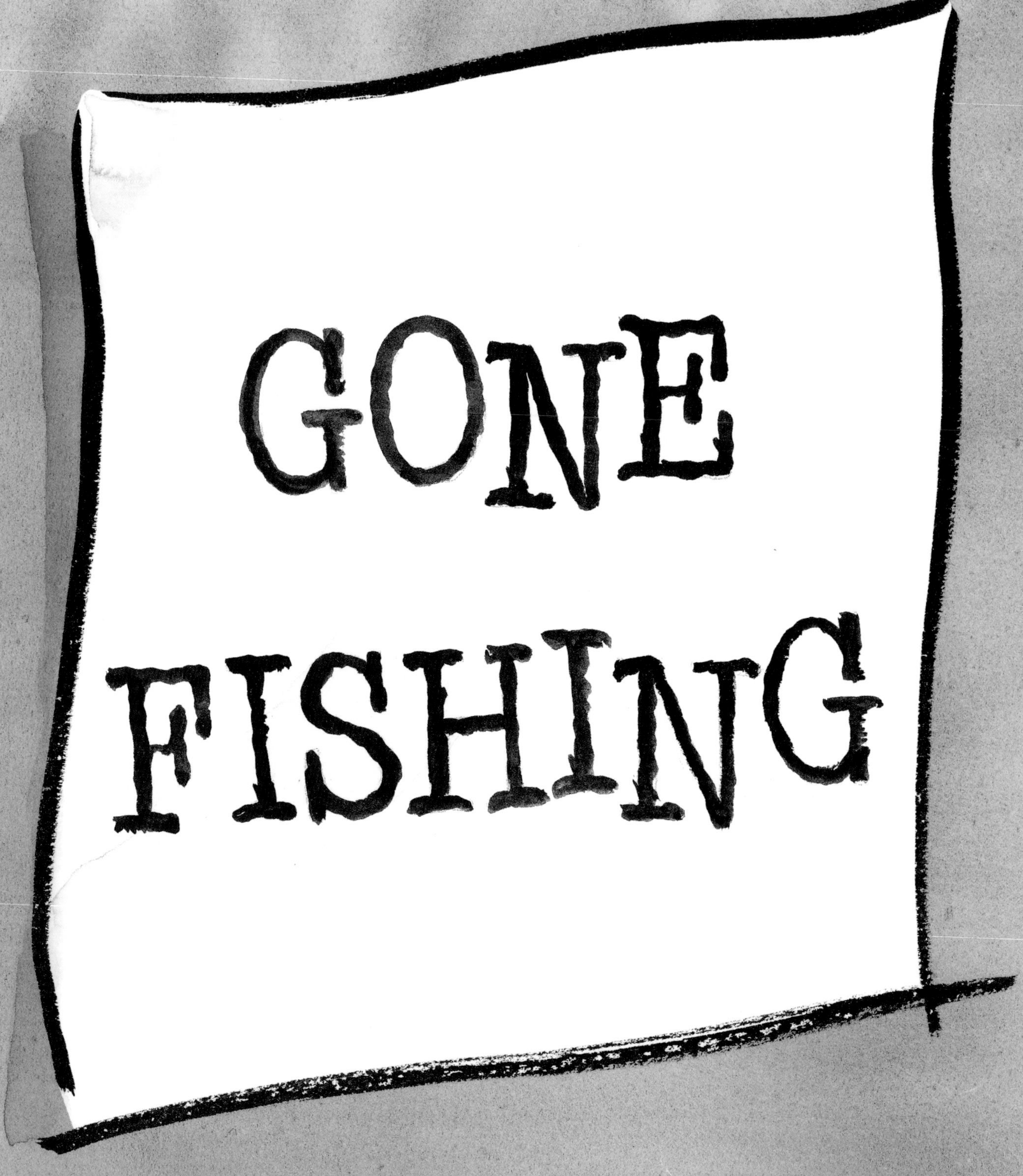
GONE
FISHING

All the animals

go to the shore.

10 buckets lined up in a row.

10 fish ready to go.

3

2

One sleepy farmer rubs his eyes
and wakes up to a fishy surprise!

For Julia
—D. C.

To Julia again, and to Grace Isabelle—
have a great childhood!
—B. L.

ISBN-13: 978-0-545-00113-7
ISBN-10: 0-545-00113-7

12 11 10 9 8 7 6 5 4 3 2 1   7 8 9 10 11 12/0

Printed in Singapore   46

First Scholastic printing, March 2007

Book design by Ann Bobco

The text for this book is set in Filosofia.

The illustrations for this book are rendered in brush and watercolor.